To..

with a heart
full of love

D1314992

Love is all around Idaho

Copyright © 2016 by Sourcebooks, Inc.
Written by Wendi Silvano
Illustrated by Joanna Czernichowska
Design by Quadrum Solutions (www.quadrumltd.com)

Sourcebooks and the colophon are registered trademarks of Sourcebooks, Inc.
All rights reserved. No part of this book may be reproduced in any form or by any electronic or
mechanical means including information storage and retrieval systems—except in the case of
brief quotations embodied in critical articles or reviews—without permission in writing from its
publisher, Sourcebooks, Inc.

Published by Sourcebooks Jabberwocky, an imprint of Sourcebooks, Inc.
P.O. Box 4410, Naperville, Illinois 60567-4410
(630) 961-3900
Fax: (630) 961-2168
www.sourcebooks.com

Source of Production: Phoenix Color, Hagerstown, Maryland
Date of Production: August 2015
Run Number: 5004410
Printed and bound in the United States of America.
PHC 10 9 8 7 6 5 4 3 2 1

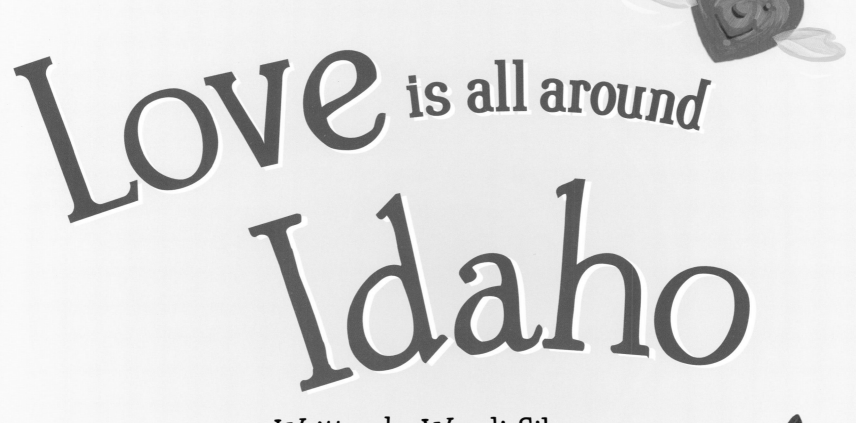

Love is all around Idaho

Written by Wendi Silvano

Illustrated by Joanna Czernichowska

sourcebooks
jabberwocky

Love is a feeling that comes from **inside.**

Everyone feels it. It can't be denied.

But how do we know that it's there? What's the clue?

How can we **see** it?

Just what can we do?

Love's all around, if you just pay attention,

in people and places too many to mention.

Go look at the park,

on the street,

at the mall.

You'll see love all over. It's big and it's small!

All around **Idaho**, in cars and on trains,
in taxis and buses, on boats and on planes,
in **Boise**, and **Nampa**,
and **Lewiston** too,
you'll find there is **love** that will come into view.

Snake River

Right there, on the lawn, in Morrison Park

is a **mom** with her **babe**,

hearing songs of a lark.

She **swaddles** him, **cuddles** him, **kisses** his ear.

That surely is **love**, it's perfectly clear!

At a store in Twin Falls, a girl gets a bear.
She **squeezes** him,
squishes him,
ruffles his hair.

It's clear that she **loves** him. She's **smiling** and bright.
She tucks him in **softly** and **gently** at night.

That same little girl, the very next day,
sees a **friend** at her school who is too **sad** to play.

So she sits down beside him and **listens** and **shares**,
making sure that he knows there's someone who **cares.**

Now the boy who was sad feels much better, you see,

so he runs home all happy to play with Magee.

They romp and they frolic.

They fetch and they run.

It's certain he loves him. They're having such fun!

You can see how **love** travels

when **shared** with a friend.

If *everyone* shares love, it never will end.

From one to another, it s p r e a d s and it **grows**.

You can't have *too much*, as everyone knows.

An officer in Caldwell who **helps** change a flat.

A Lewiston fireman who **rescues** a cat.

ALBERTSONS STADIUM

The home team that makes the crowd **cheer** and **clap**.
Each moment has **love** like a **gift** you unwrap.

There's a **father** who sits at the table each night,
helping out with the homework to get it just **right**.
He's tired and busy, but that's **love,** you know…
giving up what you want to **help** someone else **grow**.

It's not only *people* who show love, it's true.

Just come see the creatures

that play at the zoo!

The polar bear tumbles

and rolls with her cub,

and when they are finished,

she gives him a rub.

Where else is there **love?** Have we looked all around?

I think we've forgotten—love grows from the ground!

In the **mountains** and **gardens** and parks you will find

that the earth shows us **love** of all shapes and all kinds.

Wherever you look, **love** comes into sight.

It's there in the morning, it's there in the night.

But all throughout Idaho,

the best love you'll find

is a **love** that is **gentle,**

and **selfless,** and **kind...**

It's the love found at home. It shows up each day
in things people do and in things people say.
There's no greater love, I can tell you, it's true,
than the love of your family...

Especially for YOU!